WONDER BOOKS™

Mount Rushmore

A Level Three Reader

By Cynthia Klingel and Robert B. Noyed

The Child's World®

On the cover...
This picture shows Mount Rushmore from far away.

Published by The Child's World®, Inc.
PO Box 326
Chanhassen, MN 55317-0326
800-599-READ
www.childsworld.com

Photo Credits
© Charles Thatcher/Tony Stone Images: cover
© David Ball/Tony Stone Images: 29
© Deneve Feigh Bunde/Unicorn Stock Photos: 5
© Fred D. Jordan/Unicorn Stock Photos: 21
© Glen Allison/Tony Stone Worldwide: 6
© Hulton Getty: 26
© Jean Higgins/Unicorn Stock Photos: 10
© Karen Holsinger Mullen/Unicorn Stock Photos: 9
© Paul Chesley/Tony Stone Images: 25
© Photri, Inc.: 13, 14, 17, 18
© Randy Wells/Tony Stone Images: 22
© XNR Productions, Inc.: 3

Project Coordination: Editorial Directions, Inc.
Photo Research: Alice K. Flanagan

Library of Congress Cataloging-in-Publication Data
Klingel, Cynthia Fitterer.
Mount Rushmore / by Cynthia Klingel and Robert B. Noyed.
p. cm. — (Wonder books)
Summary: Briefly describes Mount Rushmore, its history, appearance,
and how the memorial was constructed.
ISBN 1-56766-826-7 (lib. bdg. : alk. paper)
1. Mount Rushmore National Memorial (S.D.)—Juvenile literature.
[1. Mount Rushmore National Memorial (S.D.)]
I. Noyed, Robert B.   II. Title.   III. Wonder books (Chanhassen, Minn.)

F657.R8 K55   2000
978.3'93—dc21   99-057848

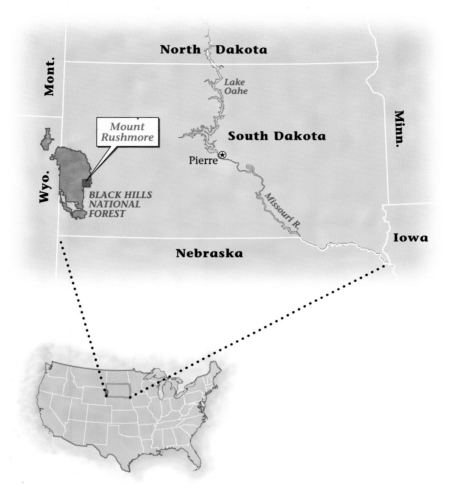

Do you know where Mount Rushmore is? Here is a map to help you find it.

There are many places to visit in the United States. Some are natural and some are man-made. One of the greatest man-made **sites** is Mount Rushmore. People from around the world travel to see Mount Rushmore.

This is the sign that many visitors →
see as they near Mount Rushmore.

Mount Rushmore is located in western South Dakota. It is part of the Black Hills region of South Dakota. Mount Rushmore is a small mountain made of **granite.**

This picture shows Mount Rushmore lit up by the sun at dawn.

The faces of George Washington, Thomas Jefferson, Abraham Lincoln, and Theodore Roosevelt are carved in the rock. The faces are very big. Each one is about 60 feet (18.3 meters) tall, or as high as a six-story building!

These visitors are looking at Mount Rushmore from far away. →

10

The faces were finished one at a time. The first face was of George Washington. Washington was the first president of the United States.

The second face to be finished was of Thomas Jefferson. Jefferson was the third president of the United States. He wrote the **Declaration of Independence.**

Here you can see the detail in the face of Thomas Jefferson.

14

The third face to be finished was of Abraham Lincoln. Lincoln was the sixteenth president of the United States. He was president during the **Civil War.** He ended **slavery** in the United States.

This picture shows Abraham Lincoln's part of the mountain.

The fourth face to be finished was of Theodore Roosevelt. Roosevelt was the twenty-sixth president of the United States. He created the first national parks in the United States.

Workers were even able to carve Theodore Roosevelt's glasses into the mountain.

16

Mount Rushmore was carved by a man named Gutzon Borglum. Borglum was born in Idaho. He was an artist and learned to carve stone in Paris, France. He carved many important statues.

← Behind this statue of Gutzon Borglum is a reflection of Mount Rushmore.

Borglum was asked to carve something very large in the Black Hills. Borglum wanted to remember four of this country's important leaders. He had to work hard to raise the money for his work. At first, not many people wanted him to do it.

This picture shows what Mount Rushmore looks like from Gutzon Borglum's studio. →

Borglum didn't give up. He convinced people that he should do the carving. He was able to raise almost $1 million to do the work. That was a lot of money in the 1920s.

In this picture, it is easy to see how carefully the faces were carved.

Borglum started working on Mount Rushmore in 1927. The face of Washington was finished in 1930. Jefferson was finished in 1936. Lincoln was finished in 1937.

This picture shows a side view of George Washington's head. →

Borglum died in March of 1941. He had not finished the face of Roosevelt. Borglum's son, Lincoln, completed the work. Roosevelt's face was finished in October of 1941.

This picture shows workers carving the faces on Mount Rushmore.

The carvings on Mount Rushmore are amazing. The carved faces look just like pictures of the presidents. They are a wonderful way to remember four important people in the history of the United States.

These visitors are looking at Mount Rushmore from the bottom of the mountain. →

29

Glossary

Civil War (SIH-vill WAR)
The Civil War happened in the United States between 1861 and 1865. During this war, the northern and southern states fought against each other.

Declaration of Independence (deh-kler-AY-shun of in-dee-PEN-dens)
The Declaration of Independence was a document written in 1776. It said that the United States was free from Great Britain.

granite (GRA-nit)
Granite is a very hard rock used for buildings and monuments. Mount Rushmore is made of granite.

sites (SITES)
Sites are places where something is found or where something took place.

slavery (SLAY-ver-ee)
Slavery is the practice of owning another person. Before the Civil War, many black people were forced to work as slaves in the southern United States.

Index

To Find Out More

Books

Curlee, Lynn. *Rushmore.* New York: Scholastic, 1999.

Gabriel, Luke S. *Mount Rushmore: From Mountain to Monument.* Chanhassen, Minn.: The Child's World, 2001.

Owens, Tomas S. *Mount Rushmore.* New York: Rosen Publishing Group, 1998.

Rey, Margret, and H. A. Rey (illustrator). *Curious George and the Hot Air Balloon.* Boston: Houghton Mifflin Company, 1998.

Web Sites

Area Parks.com, Mount Rushmore National Memorial
http://www.areaparks.com/mountrushmore/
For information about the geology, wildlife, and history of the memorial.

The National Park Service, Mount Rushmore National Memorial
http://www.nps.gov/moru/
For information about visiting Mount Rushmore.

Note to Parents and Educators

Welcome to The Wonders of Reading™! These books provide text at three different levels for beginning readers to practice and strengthen their reading skills. Additionally, the use of nonfiction text provides readers the valuable opportunity to *read to learn*, not just to learn to read.

These leveled readers allow children to choose books at their level of reading confidence and performance. Level One books offer beginning readers simple language, word choice, and sentence structure as well as a word list. Level Two books feature slightly more difficult vocabulary, longer sentences, and longer total text. In the back of each Level Two book are an index and a list of books and Web sites for finding out more information. Level Three books continue to extend word choice and length of text. In the back of each Level Three book are a glossary, an index, and a list of books and Web sites for further research.

State and national standards in reading and language arts emphasize using nonfiction at all levels of reading development. The Wonders of Reading™ fill the historical void in nonfiction material for the primary grade readers with the additional benefit of a leveled text.

About the Authors

Cindy Klingel has worked as a high school English teacher and an elementary teacher. She is currently the curriculum director for a Minnesota school district. Writing children's books is another way for her to continue her passion for sharing the written word with children. Cindy Klingel is a frequent visitor to the children's section of bookstores and enjoys spending time with her many friends, family, and two daughters.

Bob Noyed started his career as a newspaper reporter. Since then, he has worked in communications and public relations for more than fourteen years for a Minnesota school district. He enjoys writing books for children and finds that it brings a different feeling of challenge and accomplishment from other writing projects. He is an avid reader who also enjoys music, theater, traveling, and spending time with his wife, son, and daughter.